# NIGHT IS COMING

W. NIKOLA-LISA

ILLUSTRATED BY JAMICHAEL HENTERLY

DUTTON CHILDREN'S BOOKS   NEW YORK

Published in the United States by
Dutton Children's Books,
a division of Penguin Books USA Inc.

Designer: Susan Phillips

Printed in Hong Kong by South China Printing Co.
First Edition    10 9 8 7 6 5 4 3 2 1

*Library of Congress Cataloging-in-Publication Data*
Nikola-Lisa, W.
Night is coming/by W. Nikola-Lisa; illustrated by
Jamichael Henterly.
p.   cm.
Summary: Describes the sights, sounds, and
sensations of the coming of night to the countryside.
ISBN 0-525-44687-7
[1. Night—Fiction.   2. Country life—Fiction.]
I. Henterly, Jamichael, ill.   II. Title.
PZ7.N5855Ni 1991
[E]—dc20      90-3806  CIP  AC

To Dorothy E. and William H.
W. N.-L.

For my grandfathers
J. H.

Night is coming,
and out of the rustle
of Grandpa's wheat,
you can hear the whippoorwill's
hollow song arising.

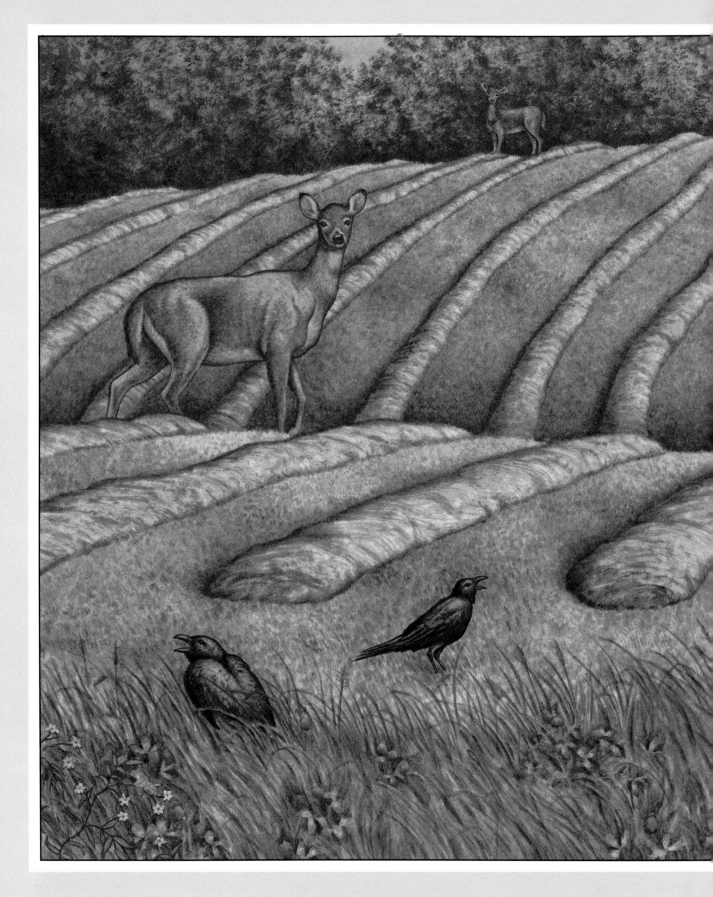

Out in the fields you can smell wild clover

mixing with the scent of freshly mown hay.

And if you stay very still
and squint way up high,
beneath the straying clouds
you'll catch the glimmer
of a red-tailed hawk
endlessly circling.

Night is coming,
and beyond the outline of Grandpa's hickory

you can see the sun glowing like a jack-o'-lantern.

If you close your eyes and listen,
you'll hear the clang
of Ginger's brass bell—
bringing in the cows,
ringing in the night.

On Grandpa's pond where the tall grasses grow,

you'll see mountains floating upside down—
like ships the color of evening.

Night is coming,
and out among the wildflowers
at the edge of Grandpa's farm,
you can hear the lambs bleating
as they nestle warm and close.

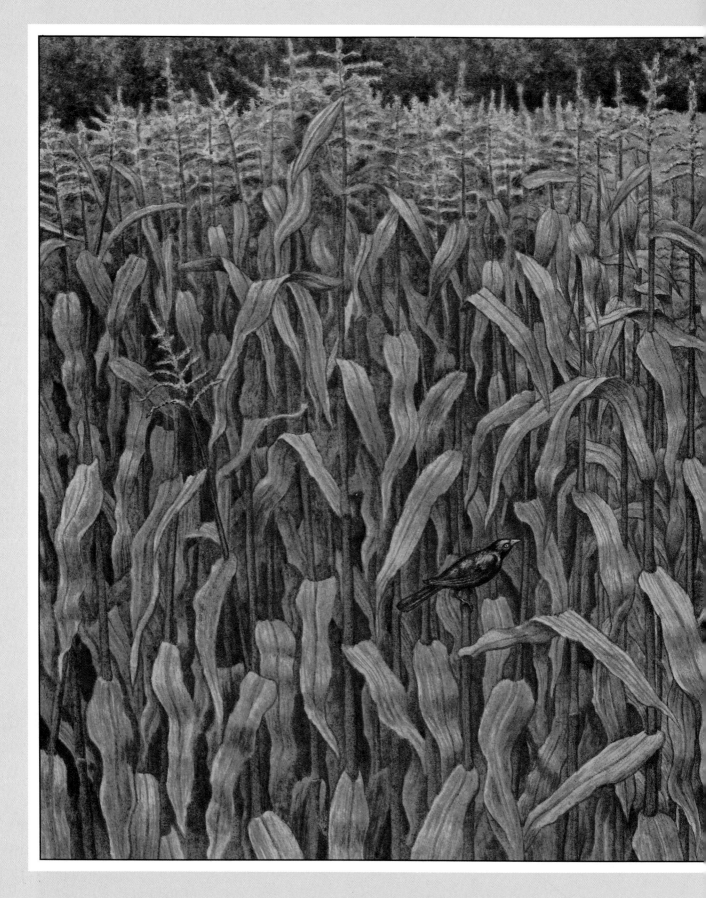

Out in the meadow where Grandpa's corn bristles,

you can see a lonely scarecrow welcoming the night.

And if you follow the road
to Grandpa's farmhouse,
to the worn, dusky porch,
you can see Grandpa waiting,
watching.

I wait too,
lulled by the rocker
creaking 'gainst the floor,
cooled by the breeze
sifting through the willow.

Night is coming,
creeping through the forest,

slipping through the valley,
silencing the day.

Night is coming.
Still are the feet.

Night is coming.
Quiet is the land.

Night is coming.
Calm is the heart.

Night is coming.

Is coming.

Is.